Patty Cat

Barbara deRubertis
Illustrated by Benton Mahan

The Kane Press
New York

Cover Design: Sheryl Kagen

Library of Congress Catalog Card Number: 96-75011

ISBN 1-57565-000-2

10 9 8 7 6 5 4 3

First published in the United States of America in 1997 by The Kane Press.
Printed in Mexico.

LET'S READ TOGETHER is a registered trademark of The Kane Press.

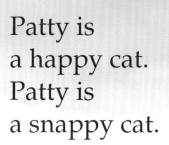

Patty is
a happy cat.
Patty is
a snappy cat.

Patty has
a brand new hat.
Patty has
a ball and bat.

Patty bats
the ball to Hal.
Hal is Patty
Cat's pal.

Patty says, "Now
pass it back."
Patty snaps
the bat....SMACK!

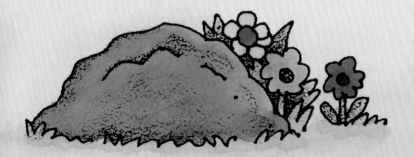

Patty's fast!
See Patty dash!

8

See Patty Cat
and Hal crash!

Patty hands
her pal the bat.
Hal taps
Patty's bat.

Hal taps.
Patty pats.
Tap...tap.
Pat...pat.

Here it comes!
The ball is fast!
Hal *smacks* the ball!
What a BLAST!

13

Back, back,
goes Patty Cat.
Fast, fast,
goes Hal the Cat.

Hal calls back
to Patty Cat,
"Patty, look!
It's Max the Rat!"

Max the Rat
grabs Patty's bat.
But Patty cannot
catch that rat.

Come back, Max!
Don't be so bad!
Look at Patty!
Patty's mad!

19

Patty Cat and
Hal are sad.
Why does Max
the Rat act bad?

Hal and Patty
have a chat.
"What shall we do
to get the bat?"

21

Patty thinks that
Max acts bad
because he's feeling
very sad.

"Max the Rat has
no *cat* pals.
Max the Rat has
no *rat* pals.

22

"We **can** fix that!"
says Patty Cat.
"We can play
with Max the Rat!"

Patty talks to
Max the Rat.
"Will you please
bring back my bat?"

Patty adds,
"And if you do,
Hal and I will
play with you."

Max the Rat gives
back the bat.
He hands the bat
to Patty Cat.

Max gives Hal
and Patty sacks.
In the sacks are
apple snacks!

Max says, "I
apologize
for acting bad.
It was not wise."

Patty's happy.
Hal is glad.
And Max the Rat
does not feel sad!

Happy, happy
Max the Rat
plays ball with Hal
and Patty Cat!